D1318501

DREAMWORKS

SHREK THE THIRD

Royally Wrong

Adapted by Annie Auerbach

HarperEntertainment
An Imprint of HarperCollins Publishers

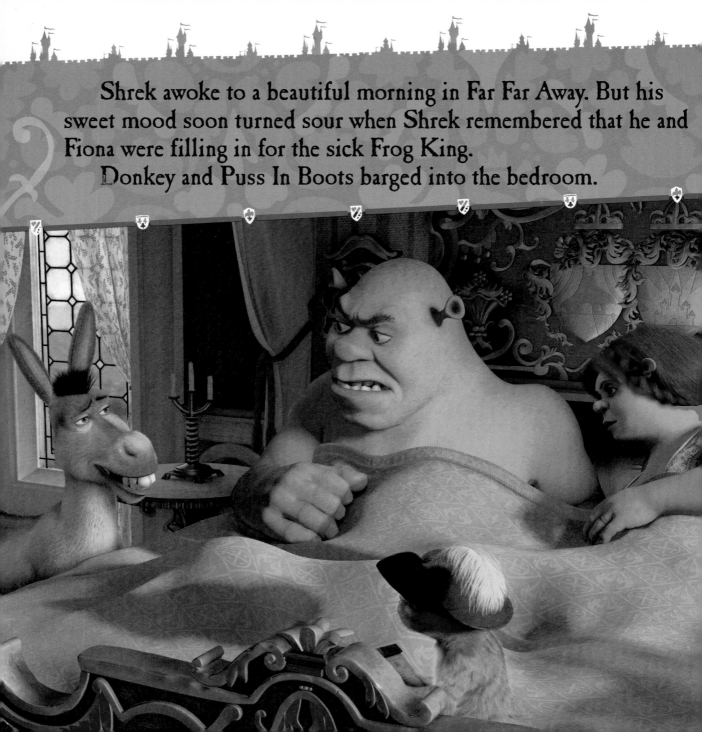

Shrek awoke to a beautiful morning in Far Far Away. But his sweet mood soon turned sour when Shrek remembered that he and Fiona were filling in for the sick Frog King.

Donkey and Puss In Boots barged into the bedroom.

"Sleepyhead," Donkey called to Shrek. "It's time to clock in. Your assistants are here to make sure all your appointments go as royal as jelly."

Shrek sighed as he got out of bed, thinking about how he'd like to make jelly out of Donkey and Puss for getting him up so early.

It was a very busy day . . . and nothing went as planned. At the knighting ceremony, Fiona watched as Shrek accidentally wounded the guest of honor with a sword. Then the royal couple went to the docks to celebrate the king's new boat. But instead of launching the boat out into the water, Shrek sank it!

Next Shrek and Fiona visited Ye Olde Lady of the Shoe elementary school. Shrek read the class a book. "My, what big teeth you have, Grandmother." Shrek said in his very best

"And then the Wolf said, *'Arrgghhh!!!'*"

"Arrgghhh!" was right. The children were so scared, they sobbed uncontrollably.

Donkey and Puss looked at each other and shook their heads. Poor Shrek—it was another royal disaster.

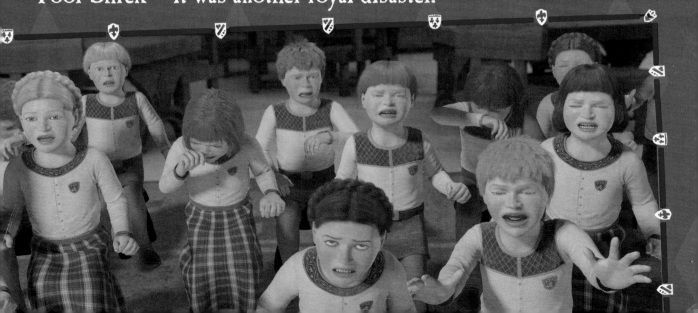

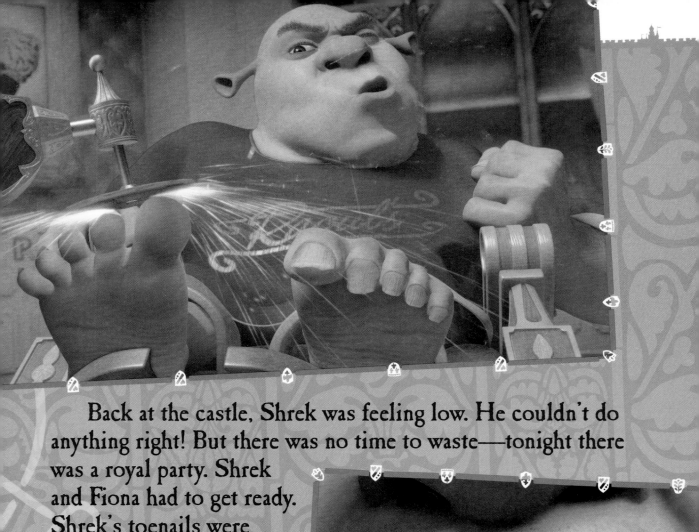

Back at the castle, Shrek was feeling low. He couldn't do anything right! But there was no time to waste—tonight there was a royal party. Shrek and Fiona had to get ready. Shrek's toenails were filed down, lipstick was applied, and a big, white wig was put on his head.

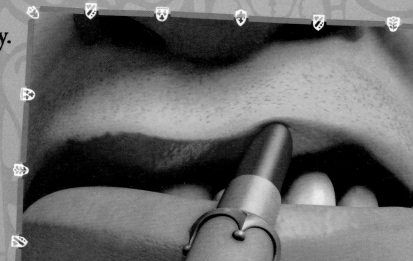

Then Fiona's nose hairs were plucked, and she was squeezed into a dress with a big silly collar. Not only did the two ogres look ridiculous, they *felt* ridiculous.

Soon it was party time. The guests were announced as they
arrived. Shrek and Fiona stood backstage, waiting to be called.

"I don't know how much longer I can keep up this act, Fiona,"
Shrek whispered.

"It's just until Dad gets better," Fiona said. Then she smiled.
"Shrek . . . you look handsome."

That made Shrek feel better. He tried to give
Fiona a kiss, but he couldn't. His outfit was too tight!

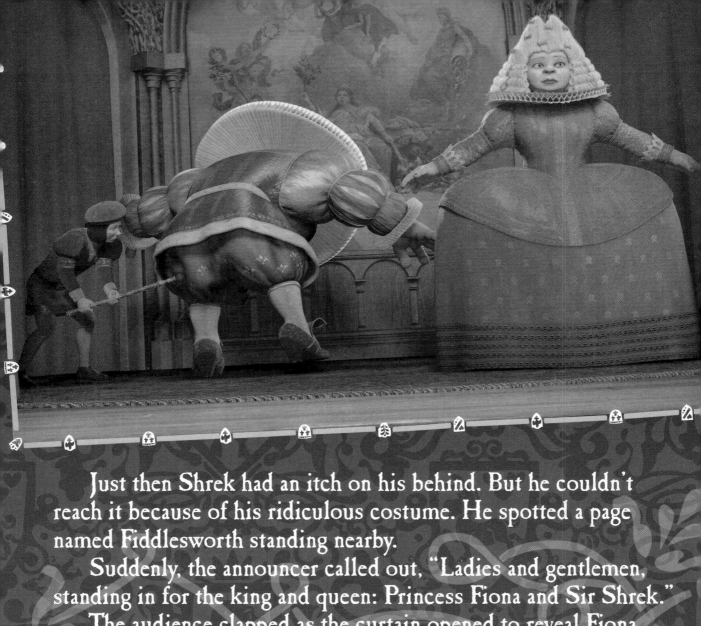

Just then Shrek had an itch on his behind. But he couldn't reach it because of his ridiculous costume. He spotted a page named Fiddlesworth standing nearby.

Suddenly, the announcer called out, "Ladies and gentlemen, standing in for the king and queen: Princess Fiona and Sir Shrek."

The audience clapped as the curtain opened to reveal Fiona . . . and Shrek, getting his behind scratched!

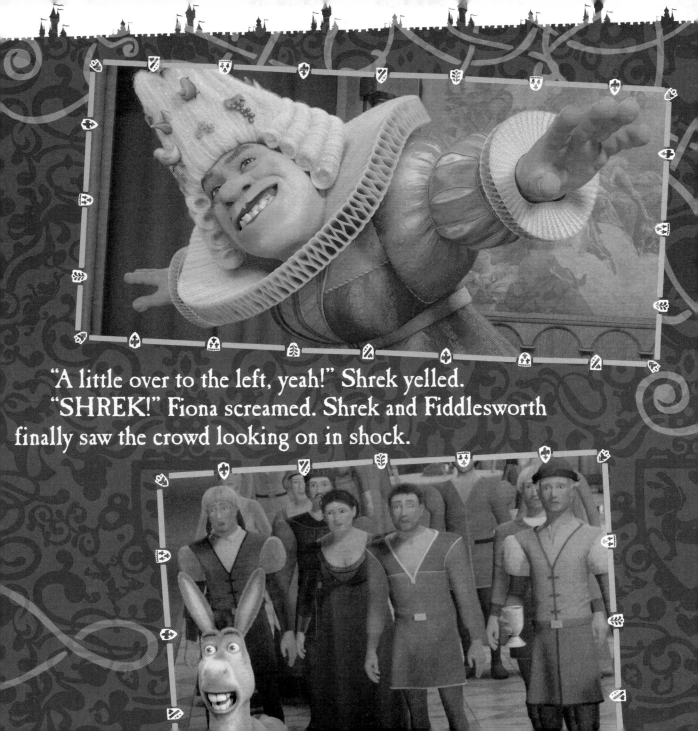

"A little over to the left, yeah!" Shrek yelled.

"SHREK!" Fiona screamed. Shrek and Fiddlesworth
finally saw the crowd looking on in shock.

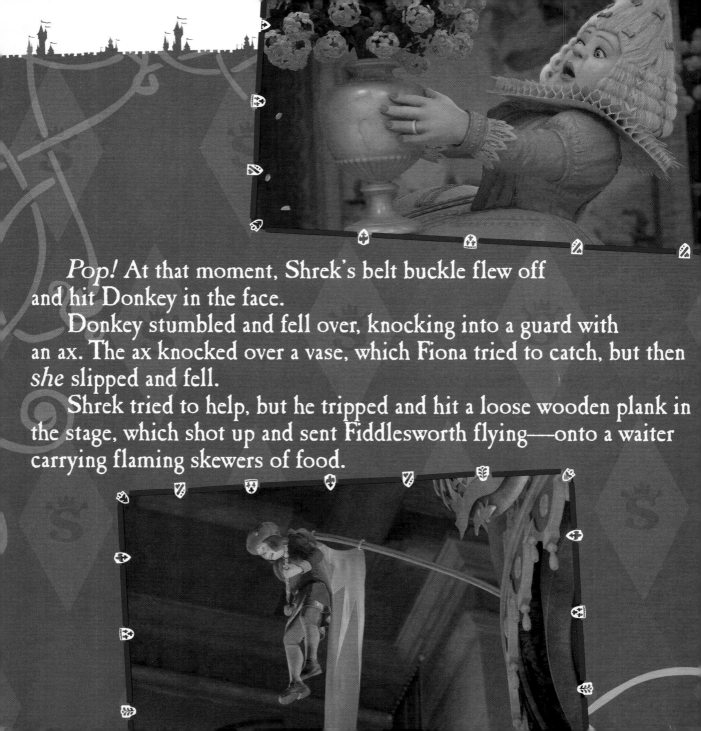

Pop! At that moment, Shrek's belt buckle flew off and hit Donkey in the face.

Donkey stumbled and fell over, knocking into a guard with an ax. The ax knocked over a vase, which Fiona tried to catch, but then *she* slipped and fell.

Shrek tried to help, but he tripped and hit a loose wooden plank in the stage, which shot up and sent Fiddlesworth flying——onto a waiter carrying flaming skewers of food.

Whoosh! The fiery food landed on the curtains, setting them ablaze. Soon the fire reached the ceiling. Finally a huge shield came tumbling down, breaking the stage in half. *Crash!* The party was over.

"That's it! We're leaving the kingdom!" Shrek insisted, when they were back in their bedroom.

"Just think," Fiona said softly, "a couple more days and we'll be back in our vermin-filled shack, filled with the rotting stench of mud and neglect." Shrek smiled at the thought.

Just then there was a knock at the door. "Somebody better be dying," Shrek growled.

Unfortunately, somebody *was* dying: King Harold.
Lying on his lily pad, the king told Fiona and Shrek the news.
The kingdom needed a new king, and Shrek was next in line.
Shrek panicked. "There's got to be somebody else," he said
hopefully.

"Aside from you, there is only one remaining heir," said
the king. With a final breath, he muttered, "Fiona's cousin.
His name is . . . Arthur."
Then the king was gone.
Shrek hung his head and comforted Fiona.

Shrek, along with Donkey and Puss, immediately set out on a quest to find Arthur. Everyone gathered at the docks to say good-bye.

"Trust me," Shrek told Fiona, "Your cousin, Arthur, will make a great king."
It seemed like the perfect job for anyone but him.

As the boat set sail, Shrek watched Far Far Away fade into the distance.

He would find Arthur and bring him back. He would return to the swamp with Fiona. He would get his happily-ever-after—something a lot less royal . . . and a lot more ogre.